Editor: Kaye We

MEET MARY KATE

Mary Kate is four years old. She lives in the country with her Mummy and Daddy and her dog Jacky, and these stories are about the things that happen to her day by day. Some of them are rather special, like the time she rescued Mummy from the loft; and some are quite ordinary, like the day she woke up with a chill and had to stay in bed; but all of them are happy stories told with that particular quality of astonishment which makes almost every happening in a young child's life seem like an adventure.

To be read aloud to children who want to hear about other boys and girls.

Cover design by Shirley Hughes

MEET MARY KATE

HELEN MORGAN

ILLUSTRATED BY SHIRLEY HUGHES

PUFFIN BOOKS

Puffin Books, Penguin Books Ltd, Harmondsworth, Middlesex, England
Penguin Books, 625 Madison Avenue, New York, New York 10022, U.S.A.
Penguin Books Australia Ltd, Ringwood, Victoria, Australia
Penguin Books Canada Ltd, 2801 John Street, Markham, Ontario, Canada L3R 1B4
Penguin Books (N.Z.) Ltd, 182–190 Wairau Road, Auckland 10, New Zealand

—

First published by Faber & Faber 1963
Published in Puffin Books 1965
Reprinted 1967, 1972, 1978

—

—

Made and printed in Great Britain
by Hazell Watson & Viney Ltd,
Aylesbury, Bucks
Set in Linotype Granjon

FOR MEGAN

CONTENTS

POOR PUSSY PIPKIN

It was the night before Mary Kate's birthday. As Mummy tucked her up in bed she said, 'This is the last time you'll go to bed three, Mary Kate. When you wake up in the morning you'll be four.'

Mary Kate pulled her old rag doll under the bedclothes with her. 'I wonder if the postman will bring me any presents?' she said.

'I expect he will,' smiled Mummy. 'Parcels and cards. He'll be ringing the bell tomorrow, you'll see.'

When Mummy had kissed her good night and gone downstairs, Mary Kate cuddled her rag doll and thought about the cake she had seen on the larder shelf. It had pink icing on it. She wondered if there would be four candles for tomorrow. Soon she was fast asleep with the rag doll tucked under her chin.

When she woke up the sun was poking its finger

through the gap in the curtains and pointing at something in the middle of the room.

It was a shining, new, blue doll's pram. Mary Kate scrambled out of bed as soon as she saw it. She was so excited she forgot all about her dressing-gown and slippers.

The pram had a blue silk pillow with lace edging and a blue silk cover to match. Under the cover was a pink woolly blanket and a soft white mattress.

Mary Kate fetched her black doll, Bobo, from the window-sill and put him in the pram. Then she put Teddy and Og, the golly, in too and began to push them gently across the room.

She was just going to give the old rag doll a ride when the door opened and Mummy looked in.

'Many Happy Returns of the Day,' said Mummy, hugging Mary Kate. Daddy put his head round the door.

'Hallo, birthday girl,' he said. 'Want to see what I've got for you?'

Mary Kate ran to see what Daddy was holding behind his back. It was a beautiful doll, with curly golden hair. It was wearing a pink frilly dress and white shoes and socks.

'Oh, isn't she lovely!' cried Mary Kate, holding her up for Mummy to see.

Then she took all the old toys out of the pram and put the new doll into it.

'I shall call her Dorabella,' she said. 'May I put her in the garden in her pram, Mummy, like the baby next door?'

'After breakfast,' Mummy promised.

'Good,' said Mary Kate. 'Then Granny will see her as soon as she comes.'

Mary Kate was washing her hands ready for lunch when Granny arrived.

'Happy Birthday, Mary Kate,' said Granny when Mary Kate came downstairs. 'That's a funny-looking baby you've got in your pram, isn't it?'

Mary Kate was surprised. 'That's my new dolly,' she said. 'Her name's Dorabella. Daddy gave her to me. Don't you like her?'

'Hmm,' said Granny. 'She didn't look like a new dolly to me. I think the fairies must have been at her. I should go and have a look, if I were you.'

Mary Kate ran at once to look in the doll's pram — but Dorabella wasn't there. She was lying on the blue silk cover on the garden seat. In her place in the pram was a little black kitten. Round his neck was a red ribbon and a card which said, 'I come with love from Granny. My name is Pipkin.'

At first Jacky, the dog, didn't like Pipkin at all. He growled whenever the kitten went near him. If Mary Kate made a fuss of Pipkin, Jacky curled up in his basket and sulked.

One morning Jacky was sulking in his basket in the kitchen while the kitten played with one of his biscuits, patting it across the floor with his little velvety paw and then pouncing on it, pretending it was a mouse.

Mummy was washing up the breakfast things and Mary Kate was drying the spoons for her. Suddenly Pipkin sent the biscuit rolling right across the kitchen. It stopped near Jacky's basket and Jacky jumped out and ate it.

'Oh, poor pussy Pipkin!' said Mummy. 'We shall have to buy you a rubber mouse to play with. Jacky won't be able to eat *that*!'

'I'll give him my old rag doll,' Mary Kate said. 'She really is very shabby now and she's so old that her face is all rubbed off.'

'Well,' said Mummy, 'if you're quite *sure* you don't want her any more. . . .'

'I'm *quite* sure,' Mary Kate told her. 'I don't take

her to bed now, not since Auntie Peggy sent me my cuddly Panda for my birthday. Pussy Pipkin can have her. I'll fetch her now,' and she went upstairs to find the rag doll.

Pipkin sniffed at the doll uncertainly. Then he patted her face with his curled-up paw. When he found she wouldn't play with him he opened his little pink mouth and bit her!

Jacky crouched in his basket watching the kitten. As soon as Pipkin came near him with the doll he snatched it up from the floor, dropped it into his basket and sat on it.

'Oh, you bad dog!' cried Mary Kate, taking him by the collar and trying to pull him out of the basket.

Jacky stayed where he was. Mary Kate could not make him move.

'Leave him for now,' said Mummy. 'Give Pipkin some milk. Jacky will soon get used to having him in the house and then he won't be so jealous.'

Mary Kate fetched Pipkin's little dish from the cupboard and put it on the floor. The kitten went to look at it and so did Jacky.

'Go away, Jacky,' said Mary Kate, carefully lifting the blue and white jug down from the table. 'Get back into your basket. This is Pipkin's milk.'

Jacky put his tail between his legs and went under the table. Pipkin began quickly to lap up the milk, flicking little drops all over his small black face. When he had had enough he sat down a little way from the dish and began to wash himself.

Up jumped Jacky and drank the rest of the milk before Mary Kate could take the dish away. Then he went back to his basket, put his nose between his paws and pretended to be asleep.

Mummy finished the washing up and Mary Kate put away the knives and forks and spoons in the table drawer. Pipkin stopped washing himself and tippy-toed round the kitchen looking for something to do.

Presently he came across the enamel bowl that held Jacky's drinking water. It was a deep bowl because Jacky was a splashy dog and made a mess on the floor if he had his water in a shallow dish.

Pipkin was far too small to see what was in the

bowl, so he stood up on his hind legs, put his front paws on the rim and peeped over the edge. He could not reach the water because Jacky had had a long drink that morning and there wasn't much left. Pipkin stretched his neck and put his head right over the side of the bowl.

Jacky sat in his basket, watching him. Then he stood up and went quickly across the kitchen. He bent his head, put his nose behind the kitten and gave him a push!

'Mia-ow!' wailed poor pussy Pipkin and over the side of the bowl he went, head first into the cold water.

'You bad dog!' scolded Mummy as she lifted up the wet and struggling kitten and began to dry him on a towel.

Mary Kate said nothing. She looked at Jacky and then at Mummy and suddenly she began to laugh.

Mummy laughed too.

Jacky wagged his tail. He was rather pleased with himself.

'We shouldn't really laugh at him,' Mummy said, 'but it *was* rather funny, wasn't it?'

QUACKETY DUCK GOES FOR A SWIM

One morning at breakfast Mummy said, 'Granny hasn't been feeling very well for a day or two, so I think we'll go and see her this afternoon and cheer her up, shall we?'

'Oh, yes,' said Mary Kate. 'Shall we take her some flowers out of the garden?'

Mummy thought that was a very good idea, so as soon as the breakfast things were washed up she and Mary Kate went into the sunny garden to pick the flowers.

'We'll pick the ones that are growing on the shady side,' said Mummy, 'and I'll stand them in the blue pitcher in a cool place till it's time for us to go out.'

When they had picked a big bunch of flowers and put them in water Mummy decided to make a cake for Granny.

'Could you make a sponge cake with lemon curd in it?' asked Mary Kate. 'Granny will like that.'

'All right,' said Mummy, 'and if there's time I'll put lemon icing on top.'

Mummy made the cake and it was quite cool by lunch time, so she iced it and put it in the larder to set.

After lunch Mary Kate went upstairs to have her rest and Mummy cleared away and washed up.

Jacky, the dog, was in the kitchen playing with one of his biscuits. He tossed it into the air and caught it in his mouth. Sometimes he didn't catch it and it rolled across the floor. Then he chased it and growled at it and snatched it up again.

When the washing-up was done, Mummy cleaned Mary Kate's shoes and put them under a chair. Then she washed her hands and went upstairs to get ready to go out.

Presently Mary Kate came one-step-two-step hopping down the stairs, dressed in a clean frock and clean socks, but wearing her slippers.

She went into the kitchen, sat down in her little chair and began to put her shoes on.

She put the left shoe on and pulled the laces tight ready for Mummy to tie. Then she tried to put the right shoe on but her foot wouldn't go in.

'Mummy,' she cried, 'my foot's too big for this shoe!'

'It can't be,' said Mummy and she loosened the laces and tried to squeeze Mary Kate's heel down.

'Push,' she said. 'You must be able to get your foot in more than that, surely?'

'No, I can't,' grunted Mary Kate. 'I can feel the end with my toes. They're all bent.'

'That's very odd,' Mummy said. 'Let me look.'

She took the shoe off and looked inside it. 'There's something in it,' she said, tipping it upside down.

Out fell Jacky's biscuit!

'No wonder you couldn't get it on!' laughed Mummy. 'There wasn't room in it for you *and* a biscuit!'

'Are we taking Jacky with us?' asked Mary Kate when her shoe was tied at last.

Mummy shook her head. 'Granny's cat doesn't like him,' she said. So they shut Jacky in the kitchen and set off down the garden towards the gate that led into the little wood.

Mummy was carrying her basket with the flowers in it and Mary Kate was carrying Quackety, her rubber duck.

The short cut to Granny's took them across a little bridge over a stream and Mary Kate thought Quackety would like to see the real ducks if they happened to be swimming near the bridge.

When they reached the stream they stopped and Mummy looked in her basket for the bag of bread-crumbs she had brought with her.

'Oh dear,' she said as soon as she put her hand into the basket. 'Do you know what I've done – I've come without Granny's cake!'

'Go back for it,' said Mary Kate. 'I'll stay here and wait for you. Perhaps the ducks will come while you're gone.'

'All right,' agreed Mummy. 'I'll be as quick as I can. Don't go on, now. Stay on the bridge till I come back.'

She gave Mary Kate the bag of crumbs, put her basket down and hurried back along the footpath towards the wood and the garden gate.

Mary Kate leaned over the rail of the bridge to wait for the ducks. Presently she saw them swimming slowly round a bend in the stream. She took some crumbs from the bag and dropped them down into the water.

As the ducks came closer to the bridge Mary Kate threw more and more bread down to them. She leaned over the rail to watch them gobbling the crumbs and suddenly Quackety leaped from under her arm and went down, down, down into the water with a SPLASH!

At the same moment Jacky ran on to the bridge, wagging his tail and panting. He jumped up at Mary Kate and began to bark. All the ducks swam quickly away, quacking loudly ... all except poor Quackety, who was bobbing up and down on the rough water and saying nothing at all.

Mary Kate pushed Jacky away and looked along the footpath. There was Mummy, hurrying towards her and carrying Granny's cake.

'He ran out as soon as I opened the kitchen door,' she called. 'We'll have to take him with us after all.' Mary Kate wasn't listening. She was peering down at the stream. 'I've lost Quackety,' she wailed. 'He jumped into the water when I was feeding the ducks.'

'Oh dear, I'm afraid you *have* lost him,' said

Mummy, coming to look. 'I don't think I can reach him, even with a stick.'

She put Granny's cake into the basket and went to the end of the bridge. There was a gap between the rail and the hedge and the bank was not steep. Mummy searched along the hedge till she found the right sort of stick and then squeezed through the gap and slithered down the bank to the edge of the stream. She stooped down and stretched out towards the rubber duck, but as soon as she touched him with the stick Quackety bobbed away from her.

All the real ducks were out of sight by now and only Quackety was left floating on the ruffled water. Every time he came near enough Mummy tried to hook him with the crooked stick but it was no use. He simply would not let her catch him.

At last Mummy stood up and called out to Mary Kate on the bridge. 'It's no good, I'm afraid,' she said. 'I just can't get hold of him.'

'He doesn't want to come,' said Mary Kate sadly. 'He wants to go with the other ducks. Look – he's swimming under the bridge.'

Mummy looked. 'You're quite right,' she said. 'He's quite out of reach now.' She turned away and climbed back up the bank and on to the bridge. As she stooped to pick up the basket, Jacky began to bark. Mummy and Mary Kate looked over the rail and there was the little dog at the edge of the stream.

Just as Quackety swam under the bridge Jacky jumped into the water.

He caught the rubber duck's tail in his mouth and carried him back to the bank. Then he scrambled up to the hedge, struggled through his own small gap and ran on to the bridge. Dropping Quackety in front of Mary Kate, Jacky wagged his tail and shook himself hard.

'Now we've all had a wetting,' laughed Mummy as she and Mary Kate jumped out of the way of the splashes. 'You're a clever dog, Jacky. You shall have a piece of Granny's lemon cake for your tea.'

'Wuff,' said Jacky, pricking his ears and looking very pleased with himself.

Mary Kate bent to pat his head. 'I'm glad you came with us after all,' she said. 'I'd have lost Quackety for ever if you hadn't been here.'

A CHILL AND AUNT MARY

Mary Kate was ill. She felt shivery and headachy and her throat hurt. 'I can't eat it, Mummy,' she said, pushing away her breakfast.

'You've caught a chill,' said Mummy. 'Bed's the best place for you. I'll get you a hot-water bottle and you can go straight back upstairs.'

It was nice being back in bed, warm and cosy, but Mary Kate felt miserable because it was the very day Aunt Mary was coming to stay.

'I shan't be able to go for walks with her or show her my toys or my books or my garden or anything,' she sighed.

'Of course you will,' said Mummy. 'You'll be better long before it's time for her to go home again. I expect she'll come and sit with you, anyway, and read to you when you feel like listening. Just now the best thing you can do is to go to sleep and get well quickly.'

So Mary Kate snuggled down under the bedclothes, cuddling her hot-water bottle in its blue jacket with the red engine embroidered on it, and soon she was fast asleep.

When she woke up the room was full of sunlight. It was very quiet. Mary Kate couldn't think what had happened. Then she remembered.

'It must be quite late,' she thought. 'I wonder if Auntie Mary has come yet? Oh dear, I *do* want a drink. I'll call Mummy.'

Mary Kate called out in a croaky voice. 'Mummy, can I have a drink, please?' but Mummy didn't hear. She was in the kitchen, peeling potatoes.

'Mummy,' called Mary Kate again, a bit louder. 'Please can I have a drink?'

Still Mummy didn't hear her. Mary Kate waited and waited and then she tried again. 'Mummee-ee-ee ... Mumm-ee-ee-ee.'

There was no answer. 'I shall have to go downstairs,' sighed Mary Kate. She was very thirsty by now and her head was aching again. She climbed out of bed and put on her slippers and dressing-gown. Then she opened her bedroom door and went out on to the landing. She was starting to go down the stairs when she heard the dining-room door open and Aunt Mary's voice say, 'I'll just run up and peep at her and see if she's still asleep.'

'Oh, Auntie Mary,' cried Mary Kate. 'I'm awake. I want a drink. I've been calling and calling, but Mummy didn't hear me.'

'You poor lamb,' said Aunt Mary, coming up the stairs two at a time. She lifted Mary Kate up and carried her back to bed. 'I'll fetch you a drink right away,' she promised, 'and I'll bring you something else, too.' Away went Aunt Mary and presently she was back again with a mug of orange juice and the 'something else'.

It was the little bell from the dining-room

mantelpiece – a brass lady in a crinoline skirt.

'There you are, Mary Kate,' said Aunt Mary. 'No more getting out of bed and no more calling and calling and nobody coming. Just ring this bell when you want something and somebody will be here before you can say "Jack Robinson".'

'Thank you, Auntie,' Mary Kate said, putting down her empty mug. 'I think I'll just lie down again now. I feel all wishy-washy.'

'All right, pet,' said Aunt Mary. 'We won't disturb you.'

Mary Kate slept till lunch time. She ate the scrambled egg Aunt Mary brought her and then Mummy came to straighten up the bed and wash her face and hands.

'Auntie has had an idea,' said Mummy, plumping up Mary Kate's pillow, 'and we want to know what you think of it.'

'What is it?' asked Mary Kate, trying to keep quite still while Mummy smoothed the covers. It was rather difficult because a woolly blanket was tickling her nose.

'Well,' said Mummy, 'we thought we'd take your bed down into Auntie's room when Daddy comes home this evening. Would you like that?'

'Oh, yes,' said Mary Kate. 'Then you can leave the door open and I'll be able to see you.'

'That's what we thought,' smiled Mummy, 'and it will save our poor legs running up and down the stairs – and if you want anything in the night Auntie will be there to get it for you.'

When Daddy came home he came straight upstairs, lifted Mary Kate out of bed and wrapped her in her eiderdown, all nice and cosy. Then he carried her down to the little room off the dining-room where Aunt Mary always slept when she stayed with them. He put her in the big armchair with the blue velvet cushions and went to help Mummy with the bed.

Mary Kate sat and waited. Presently Aunt Mary came in, almost hidden behind a pile of blankets and sheets and with a pillow balanced on her head. She looked so funny that Mary Kate laughed and the laugh made her cough and she had to be patted on the back.

Then Mummy arrived, carrying bits of Mary Kate's bed, and behind her was Daddy with more bits.

While Mummy and Aunt Mary were upstairs fetching the mattress, Daddy began to put the bits of bed together again in the corner by the little window. At last it was quite ready. Aunt Mary put a hot-water bottle in and Mummy put Mary Kate in.

'When you feel well enough to sit up,' she said, 'you'll be able to look out of the window.'

'And when she wants to *climb* out of the window,' laughed Aunt Mary, 'we'll know she's better!'

A day or two later Mary Kate *did* feel better. Her headaches had gone and her sore throat was easier. She didn't feel so hot, but she was still rather snuffly. Being in bed began to be rather boring.

'Will you read me a story, please, Auntie?' she asked after breakfast.

'I'm sorry, pet,' said Aunt Mary, 'but it's Saturday, and I'm going to be very busy today. I'll read to you tomorrow.'

So Mary Kate asked Daddy if he would read to her, but he said he was busy, too. So did Mummy.

Mary Kate pulled the bedclothes up under her chin, feeling rather miserable.

'What are they all busy *at*?' she wondered.

Presently Aunt Mary came in. 'I've brought you a new picture book to look at,' she said.

Mary Kate was pleased. She sat up in bed and looked at the picture book and every time Mummy

or Aunt Mary went past the door they called out to her. They were both wearing big overalls and they seemed to have sacks tied round their middles. They had dusters pinned round their heads and they were carrying brooms and brushes and buckets and mops.

'Auntie, what are you doing?' called Mary Kate.

Aunt Mary laughed. 'Secrets,' she said. She had a black smut on her face and her sack pinny was all wet.

There was a great deal of noise going on overhead. Mary Kate could hear bangings and scrapings and bumps and a strange swishing sound.

Then Daddy went by in his hat and coat and Mary Kate heard the front door close.

A little later on he came back and called out from the hall. Aunt Mary, who was in the dining-room, gave a little shriek and shut Mary Kate's door quickly.

'They don't want me to see,' thought Mary Kate. 'Whatever can they be doing?'

The noises upstairs went on all the morning and all the afternoon – scraping and slapping and bumping, and Mummy and Daddy and Aunt Mary talking and laughing. Lunch was just soup and sandwiches and a banana. Every now and then someone would come and look in at Mary Kate and smile a mysterious smile. They brought her a jigsaw puzzle, a cut-out book and two little dolls to dress and undress, but they wouldn't tell her what they were doing.

'I'm sure they're in my bedroom,' she thought. When Mummy came in with her tea, Mary Kate said, 'I know what you're doing. You're spring-cleaning.'

Mummy laughed. 'Not quite,' she said, 'though we *have* done a lot of sweeping and scrubbing. We should be finished by the day after tomorrow. By then I expect you'll be well enough to go up and see what it's all about. Eat up your tea, now, there's a good girl.'

By Monday morning Mary Kate had sniffed her very last sniff, just as Mummy said she would.

'You can get up after breakfast,' Aunt Mary told her when she brought in the tray.

'Good,' said Mary Kate. 'I want to know what the secret is upstairs.'

As soon as she had finished her breakfast Mary Kate put on her dressing-gown and slippers. 'Can I go up and see the secret now?' she asked, going into the dining-room.

'Not till you've had your bath,' said Mummy. 'Auntie is running it now. Up you go.'

So Mary Kate went upstairs to the bathroom. Her legs felt rather wobbly as she climbed and she had to hold on tightly to the bannister rail. Half-way up she sat down. She could hear the taps running in the bathroom and Aunt Mary singing.

'I wonder if I could just peep into my bedroom,' she thought, 'and see what all the noise was about the other day.'

She began to creep quietly up the stairs, but just as she reached the top Aunt Mary came out of the bathroom.

'Come along, pet,' she said, lifting Mary Kate up. 'A quick bath. No ducks or boats or showers with the sponge.'

'Can't I just peep at the secret?' pleaded Mary Kate.

'Not till you're dressed,' said Aunt Mary firmly. 'We don't want you to catch another chill. Your bedroom window is wide open.'

'So it *is* in my bedroom,' thought Mary Kate as Aunt Mary lifted her into the bath. 'Whatever can it be?'

When Mary Kate was bathed and dried Aunt

35

Mary dressed her by the electric fire in Mummy's bedroom.

As soon as her shoes had been fastened Mary Kate asked, 'Can I see the secret now?'

'All right,' laughed Mummy, coming into the room. They all went across the landing and Aunt Mary flung open the door of Mary Kate's bedroom. 'Hey Presto!' she said.

Mary Kate gasped. It was no longer a pink and white room with a curtained alcove for her clothes and a chest of drawers so tall that she couldn't see the top of it. The walls were the colour of daffodils and the curtains were striped blue and white. The Stripy Tiger mat that Granny had made her was still there, but there was a new mat as well, with a red and white clown in the middle of it.

The new blue chest of drawers and dressing-table were just the right height for Mary Kate and in the alcove was a real wardrobe. She could reach to open the door herself and inside was a row of pretty coloured hangers for her clothes.

All round the room were paintings of Mary Kate's favourite story-book people and when she looked more closely she saw there were other pictures, too. Some of her toys had their portraits on the walls!

'It's Auntie Mary's birthday present to you,' Mummy told her. 'You remember she promised you something else besides the sweets she sent you? Well – this is it. We had to wait till she came to stay with us because she painted the pictures.'

'We shall have to paint your bed blue, too,' said Aunt Mary. 'We'll put you on a camp bed till it's dry and as soon as the smell of paint has worn off you can move back up here.'

'It's lovely,' said Mary Kate, hugging Aunt Mary. 'Now I know why you wanted me downstairs. You couldn't have done it with me up here. What a good thing I had a chill!'

MRS DOVER'S TUBS

IT was raining. Mummy had switched on the electric fire in the living-room and she was sitting in her favourite chair reading a magazine. Mary Kate was drawing a house, but she couldn't get it right. She meant it to be the crooked little house that the crooked man lived in, but it wouldn't come out crooked enough. At last she gave up trying and went to look over Mummy's shoulder at the magazine.

There was nothing but writing on the page Mummy was reading and Mary Kate was just going to turn away and find something else to do when Mummy turned over the page.

Mary Kate stayed to look – and there, in bright colours, was a lovely picture of a house and a beautiful garden.

'Oh,' said Mary Kate. 'Isn't that a lovely house, Mummy?'

'Yes, isn't it,' Mummy agreed. 'There are some

more pictures on the next page. Look, this is the back of the house.' She showed Mary Kate another picture.

'Oh,' cried Mary Kate. 'Mummy, look – look at this picture!' and she pointed to a small picture in the corner of the page.

'I don't see anything special,' said Mummy in a puzzled voice. 'It's only a picture of a balcony with baskets of flowers hanging from it.'

'Yes, but look what's on the balcony!' cried Mary Kate. 'Do you see? Big tub things with plants growing in them.'

Mummy looked more closely at the picture. 'Well – what's so exciting about that?' she asked.

'It's Mrs Dover,' explained Mary Kate. 'She hasn't got a garden, but she *has* got a balcony. Mummy, couldn't Mrs Dover have tubs, too?'

'Who's Mrs Dover?' asked Aunt Mary, coming in just then with the tea trolley. 'And why should she want tubs?'

'She's a friend of Granny's,' Mary Kate told her, 'and she lives at the other end of the village in the flat over the grocer's shop. We take her flowers sometimes when we go to see Granny.'

Mummy reached for the teapot and stood it down

by the electric fire. 'Mrs Dover is very old,' she said, 'and she can't get down the stairs now, so she has to stay up in her flat all the time. Her daughter lives at the back of the shop and looks after her. The flat has a little balcony overlooking the street. Mrs Dover sits there on fine afternoons watching the people. She used to be a great gardener. She has several pot plants on her window-sill, and Mary Kate takes her primroses and bluebells and whatever else we find when we go through the wood on our way to the village, and sometimes we make her up a bunch of flowers from the garden.'

'I see,' said Aunt Mary. 'And you think she could have tubs on her balcony, do you, Mary Kate?'

'Well, couldn't she?' asked Mary Kate. 'There's an old barrel in the garage. I'm sure Daddy doesn't want it. He had two and he cut one in half and made two tubs to put by the front door. Couldn't we cut the other one in half and give the tubs to Mrs Dover?'

Aunt Mary laughed. 'Not so fast, not so fast,' she said. 'Daddy might want the barrel for something.'

'I don't think he does,' said Mummy, 'but we'll ask him when he comes home. I think it's a very good idea, Mary Kate. We'll see what we can do about it. Now I must go and fetch the rest of the tea things.'

When Mummy had gone Aunt Mary said thoughtfully, 'We can't just give your friend Mrs Dover two empty tubs, you know. We shall have to plant them up for her. And they'll be very heavy when they're full of earth. How are we going to haul them up to her balcony?'

'She's got outside stairs,' said Mary Kate. 'They go right up the side of the shop and on to the balcony. George could carry the tubs up. He's very strong.'

'Who's George?' asked Aunt Mary.

'He works in the shop,' Mary Kate told her. 'He carries huge boxes of groceries about and unloads great crates of things from the vans when they come. I'm sure he could manage the tubs. They'll only be little. It's not a very big barrel, you know. Not as big as the one Daddy used for our tubs. Oh, I *do* hope he says we can have it!'

Daddy *did* say they could have it. In fact, he went out that very evening and sawed it in half. Mary Kate, cuddling her Teddy in her newly painted blue bed, heard him and smiled to herself. 'Tomorrow,' she thought, 'I'll help Auntie Mary to fill the tubs with earth and then we'll plant plants in them and take them to Mrs Dover.'

The next morning after breakfast Mary Kate went out to look at the two little tubs. When she saw them she was rather disappointed. They looked very shabby. Aunt Mary thought so too. 'We'll have to give them a coat of paint or something,' she said. 'Let's go and see what there is in the shed.'

There were several tins in the shed with little bits of paint in them. Aunt Mary looked at them all and at last she made up her mind to take the tin with the most paint – and the paint was yellow.

It took Aunt Mary all the morning to paint the two tubs. Mary Kate did a bit, too, but not much, in case she got herself in a mess. When they were finished, the tubs looked much better than they had done before, but Aunt Mary still wasn't satisfied. 'It's too much of a muchness,' she said. 'All that yellow. I'm going to look in the shed again, Mary Kate. You stay here and wiggle this brush about in this jar of turps to clean it.'

So Mary Kate knelt on the path and wiggled the paint brush about in the jam jar while Aunt Mary poked about in the shed again. Presently Aunt Mary came back with a small tin of red paint. It was a

new tin. 'We'll use this,' she said, 'and we'll buy Daddy another one when we go shopping.'

'What are you going to do with it?' asked Mary Kate. 'Are you going to make stripes on the tubs? Or spots?'

'No,' said Aunt Mary, laughing. 'You see these two iron bands that run round the tub? Well, I'm going to paint them red.'

'Well, that *is* stripes,' said Mary Kate. 'Two red stripes going right round each tub.'

'So it is,' agreed Aunt Mary. 'And I think they're going to look very nice when they're done.'

They did. Mary Kate was so pleased with them that she ran indoors to fetch Mummy.

'My goodness,' said Mummy, when she saw the tubs. 'You *have* made them look gay. They ought to cheer Mrs Dover up even if they don't have any flowers in them.'

'But they *will* have flowers,' Aunt Mary said, collecting up the paint tins and the brushes and bottles and jars. 'We'll fill the tubs with earth as soon as the paint is dry. After lunch, Mary Kate, we'll hunt about in the garden for big stones and bits of broken brick to put in the bottom of the tubs so that the water will drain properly and not make a nasty puddle on the top every time it rains.'

They filled the tubs with earth the next day and then Aunt Mary said they must look for some plants to put in them.

'We'll fill one of them with pansies,' she said. 'They go on having lots of flowers for a long time and look very pretty. We'll take one or two bits from Daddy's garden for a start and then I'll run down to the greengrocer and buy a few of those big yellow ones we saw last week.'

The tub looked lovely when it was full of pansies. Aunt Mary was rather proud of it. 'What shall we put in the other one?' she asked.

Mary Kate looked at the tub and then she looked at Aunt Mary. 'I think,' she said slowly, 'I should like to give it to Mrs Dover just as it is and give her some seeds so that she can plant them herself and watch them grow.'

'What a good idea,' cried Aunt Mary. 'You *are* a clever girl, Mary Kate. I should never have thought of that.'

Mrs Dover was delighted with her two bright tubs. She planted the seeds Mary Kate gave her, and whenever Mummy and Mary Kate went to see Granny they looked up at Mrs Dover's balcony to see how the tubs were getting on. On fine days Mrs Dover would be sitting there and she would wave her hand to them. Then, one sunny afternoon, she beckoned to them to come up and see her. They climbed the iron staircase to the balcony to see what she wanted.

'I've got something for you, Mary Kate,' the old lady said with a smile. 'Hold out your hands and shut your eyes, now.'

Mary Kate screwed up her eyes and held out her two hands quite flat.

Mrs Dover put something tickly on the palm of one hand and something small on the palm of the other.

Mary Kate opened her eyes. She was holding a toffee and a little posy of mignonette.

'I grew it myself,' said Mrs Dover, nodding towards the tubs. 'It's the first bunch of flowers I've picked from my own little round garden.'

THE SHORT CUT

AT the bottom of the garden was a little wood. It was so small that from her bedroom window Mary Kate could see right through it to the field beyond and the bridge over the stream. There was a winding path through the woods that led from the gate in the garden to the stile in the fence round the field. It was a short cut to the village and to Granny's cottage.

One Saturday afternoon Daddy and Mary Kate were in the garden pretending to do a little weeding when Mary Kate saw something shining in the grass. She bent down to pick it up.

'Daddy, look what I've found!' she called as soon as she saw what it was. 'It's Granny's brooch!'

'So it is,' said Daddy, coming to look. 'She must have dropped it when she came over with the eggs this morning. Poor Granny – she will be worried. She'll think it's lost.'

'We'll give it to her next time we see her,' said Mary Kate.

Daddy looked thoughtful. 'I think I'll take it across to her now,' he said. 'She's had it a very, very long time and she'll be upset at losing it.'

'Can I come too?' asked Mary Kate.

Daddy looked at his watch. 'I don't think there's time,' he said. 'You're supposed to be going to have your hair cut at four o'clock. Mummy will be wanting to get you ready soon. I tell you what – I'll meet you in the village about half-past four and we'll go and have tea in the Bun Shop.'

'Ooh – lovely!' cried Mary Kate. 'I'll go and tell Mummy.'

She waited till Daddy had disappeared round the bend in the path and then she went back to the house to tell Mummy what had happened.

The back door was open, but Mummy wasn't in the kitchen. She wasn't in the dining-room, either. Mary Kate went through the hall and opened the living-room door. Jacky was in there, curled up in one of the armchairs, where he wasn't supposed to be.

'Naughty dog,' said Mary Kate, scratching him behind the ears. 'You know you're not allowed to sit in this chair.'

Jacky took no notice. He was pretending to be asleep.

Mary Kate was just going to push him out of the chair when there came the sound of a loud crash from upstairs and Mummy's voice calling for Daddy.

Mary Kate ran to the bottom of the stairs. 'Mummy,' she shouted, 'what's the matter? Are you all right?' and she ran upstairs as fast as she could. When she reached the top she saw a step-ladder lying on the landing.

'I'm all right,' said Mummy's voice from over her head. 'I was just coming down from the loft when the ladder slipped. Luckily I was holding on to the rail that Daddy put up. Go and fetch him, will you?'

'I can't,' said Mary Kate, and she told Mummy about Granny's brooch.

'Oh dear,' said Mummy. 'Now what are we going to do? I can't jump down – it's too far.'

'Shall I go next door?' suggested Mary Kate.

'There's no one in,' sighed Mummy. 'I heard them all go out an hour ago.'

'Shall I go to the bungalow, then?' asked Mary Kate. 'I won't walk on the road.'

Mary Kate wasn't allowed to go out by herself yet, because buses came along the lane where she lived and a great many cars and lorries too, and the footpath was very narrow. The bungalow was a little way down the hill and there were no more houses between it and the village.

Mummy hesitated. Then – 'All right,' she said at last. 'But if there isn't any one don't go any farther. I shall just have to stay here till Daddy comes back.'

Mary Kate ran down the stairs and out into the garden. She was opening the gate to the road when she remembered something. That very morning the milkman had told her he had just seen the people from the bungalow piling their luggage into their car. They were off on their holiday!

Mary Kate was about to turn back and tell Mummy when she remembered something else. She was supposed to be having her hair cut at four o'clock and Daddy had said he would see her at the Bun Shop – so that meant he wouldn't be coming back home.

Mary Kate looked down the garden towards the gate and the path that led through the wood to Granny's. There was only one thing to do. She would have to go to Granny's by herself and fetch Daddy.

She ran into the house and called up the stairs, 'Mummy, I'm going to Granny's to fetch Daddy.' Then she ran out again without waiting to hear what Mummy said. She opened the gate at the bottom of the garden and went into the wood. It seemed rather dark under the trees after the bright, sunny garden and the little path was twistier than she remembered, and longer too. Then, at last, she saw a bit of green through the trees.

'There's the field,' she thought. 'I shall come to the fence in a minute.'

She followed the path round a big clump of bushes and there was the stile. Mary Kate climbed up to the step, scrambled over to the other side and jumped down. Soon she came to the bridge across the stream. The ducks were just swimming underneath, but there was no time to stop and look at them today.

'I must get to Granny's as fast as I can,' thought Mary Kate, running over the little humpy bridge. 'Daddy might have gone to the village already to look for Mummy and me. It must be nearly four o'clock by now.'

The path through the field on the other side of the bridge was very rough, but still Mary Kate ran as fast as she could. At last she came to the kissing-

gate in the corner of the field. She pulled it towards her and squeezed round it. She was in the narrow alley that ran along the back of the churchyard. There was a high wall on one side of her and a hedge on the other.

There were stinging-nettles all along the hedge, so Mary Kate had to go carefully. When she reached the gate in the churchyard wall she found it shut. The latch was so high up that she had to stand on tiptoe to reach it. It was very stiff. Mary Kate remembered that Mummy sometimes had to jerk it up and down to make it work. She jerked as hard as she could and then the gate swung open so suddenly that she fell through and tumbled down in a heap on the grass. She scrambled up, rather out of breath and grubby, but not hurt. She was just starting off down the flagged path that led to the main gate when she remembered that Mummy had once told her not to run in the churchyard, so she walked as fast as she could, keeping her legs very stiff and hoping it didn't look like running.

The main gate was always open, so out went Mary Kate into the village street. There was nobody about and there didn't seem to be any traffic, but she stopped and listened and looked both ways before she ran across the road and down the lane on the other side.

There was Granny's cottage and there, at the gate, was Daddy.

'Good gracious me!' he cried when he saw Mary Kate. 'Whatever are you doing here?'

'Mummy's stuck in the loft,' panted Mary Kate. 'The ladder fell down and there's nobody to pick it up, so I came to fetch you. I'm not sure if Mummy heard me say I was coming.'

'Oh, dear,' said Daddy. 'Mummy must have been looking for those books I asked her about. I'd better get home as fast as I can!'

Just then they heard the sound of the bus coming round by the church.

'I'll get the bus. Stay with Granny,' said Daddy and he dashed off down the lane to the bus stop at the corner and jumped on the bus.

Mary Kate went round the back of Granny's cottage to the kitchen door and told Granny what had happened. Granny *was* surprised. 'You'd better have a drink of lemonade and your face and hands washed,' she said, 'and then I'll take you to have your hair cut. It's just after ten to four now, so we shan't be very late.'

'Is that all it is?' said Mary Kate. 'I must have come very fast. I ran all the way – except through the churchyard. It *is* a short cut, isn't it?'

Granny laughed and washed Mary Kate's face and hands and tidied her hair.

'There – you'll do,' she said. 'I'll just put my hat and coat on while you drink your lemonade and then we'll go and get *you* a short cut. After that I'll take you home. But don't expect *me* to run all the way! My legs are far too old for that!'

THE SILVER THIMBLE

MARY KATE woke up one morning with the feeling that something rather special was going to happen. She lay quite still for a few minutes, trying to think what it could be. Then she remembered. Today was Saturday and Auntie Dot and Uncle Ned were coming for the week-end.

Mary Kate leaned over the side of her bed and lifted her best doll, Dorabella, out of the doll's cot, and began to dress her. She was just buttoning Dorabella's pinafore when she heard the alarm clock ringing and a moment or two later Mummy went downstairs.

Tucking Dorabella under her arm, Mary Kate climbed out of bed and followed Mummy down.

'Good gracious me!' cried Mummy, when she saw Mary Kate. 'There was no need for you to get up early as well. And Dorabella dressed already!'

'I put her best clothes on,' explained Mary Kate, 'because of Auntie Dot and Uncle Ned. She's wear-

ing her pinafore to keep her frock clean. She can sit quietly on my little chair until it's time to go out.'

'Is she going out, then?' asked Mummy in surprise.

'Oh, yes,' said Mary Kate. 'I told her last night she could go to the station with us to meet the train.'

'Well, I'm afraid I shan't have time to go,' Mummy said. 'I have far too much to do in the house, and I want to make one of Uncle Ned's favourite fruit and nut cakes. Daddy will have to take you.'

'All right,' said Mary Kate. 'May I have my breakfast now, please?'

'Go and put your dressing-gown on first,' Mummy said, 'and tell Daddy breakfast will be ready in ten minutes.'

After breakfast Mary Kate and Daddy went upstairs to get dressed. Mummy cleared the table and washed up and then she began to make the fruit cake.

When Mary Kate was ready except for her hat and coat she sat on a chair and waited for Daddy to finish dressing. He was just fastening his shirt when one of the buttons jumped off and rolled across the floor.

'Oh dear,' said Daddy. 'Where did that go?'

'Under the bed, I think,' Mary Kate told him – and she knelt down to look. 'I can see it,' she grunted, peering under the bed, 'but I can't reach it.'

So Daddy had to go down on the floor beside her and stretch out his long arm for the button.

'Hold it for me, Mary Kate,' he said, 'while I fasten my shoelaces. I shall have to go and ask Mummy to sew it on again.'

When the shoelaces were fastened Daddy went downstairs to Mummy's workbox, took out a needle and threaded it with white cotton. Then he took the needle into the kitchen. Mary Kate followed him, carrying the button.

Mummy wiped her floury hands on her apron.

'I must have my thimble,' she said. 'I can't sew without it. Run and fetch it for me, will you, Mary Kate?'

Mary Kate ran to Mummy's workbox and took out the silver thimble. She put it in her pocket to keep it safe, closed the workbox and went back to the kitchen.

Daddy stood quite still while Mummy sewed the button on his shirt and then he took the needle and cotton and put them away again. Mummy went on making the fruit cake, and Mary Kate put on her hat and coat and waited for Daddy in the hall.

Mummy was putting the cake mixture into the baking tin when Daddy came downstairs again. 'We're off now,' he called, fastening Mary Kate's coat properly and straightening her hat for her. 'We shan't be long.'

'All right,' called Mummy. 'Good-bye.'

'Good-bye,' shouted Mary Kate and, 'Good-bye,' said Daddy, and they set off down the hill towards the station.

They hadn't gone very far when Mary Kate suddenly remembered Dorabella.

'I forgot all about her because of the button,' she said. 'She's sitting in my little chair waiting to be taken out.'

'Oh dear,' said Daddy, looking at his watch. 'We haven't a great deal of time now. Surely she won't mind being left behind just this once, will she?'

'Yes, she will,' said Mary Kate. 'I promised her she could come with us. She'll cry if we don't take her.'

'Oh well,' sighed Daddy, 'if you promised, that's different. You wait here and I'll run back for her.'

Off he went back up the hill, while Mary Kate waited on the narrow footpath. In a minute or two Daddy came running back with Dorabella under his arm.

'You were quite right,' he said, giving her to Mary Kate. 'She looked as though she was going to cry.'

'She's still got her pinafore on,' said Mary Kate.

'Well, you'll have to take it off when we get to the station,' Daddy told her. 'We must hurry now, or Auntie Dot and Uncle Ned will be there before us.'

They hurried down the hill and arrived at the station just as the train came in. Auntie Dot was looking out of the carriage window and she waved to Mary Kate, who couldn't wave back because she was trying to unfasten Dorabella's pinafore.

Daddy went to find a taxi while Uncle Ned collected the luggage. 'I'm on holiday,' he said, 'and carrying a case uphill is too much like hard work for my liking.'

Mary Kate was very pleased. Dorabella had never been in a taxi before.

Mummy had coffee and biscuits ready for them when they got home and the fruit cake was in the oven beginning to smell spicy and nice.

'I've dropped my silver thimble somewhere,' said Mummy as she poured some milk into Mary Kate's mug. 'Will you see if you can find it for me, pet?'

Mary Kate put Dorabella into her pram and began to look for the thimble. She searched and searched but she couldn't see it anywhere. She had just stopped for a minute to drink her milk when Uncle Ned came into the kitchen.

'Mummy says you're playing "Hunt the Thimble",' he said, 'so I've come to join you.'

He moved the little cupboard and looked under the door-mat and poked behind the cooker with the broom handle. Mary Kate peered into the peg bag and peeped into the vegetable rack and the dog basket, but they couldn't find the thimble anywhere.

'Never mind,' said Mummy, coming in with the coffee tray and putting it on the table. 'I expect I shall find it when I sweep.'

She moved Mary Kate out of the way and opened the oven door to peep at the cake.

'That smells jolly good,' said Uncle Ned.

The cake *was* good. They had it for tea. Uncle

Ned had one big slice and then he had another and then he said he thought he could manage a third.

He pulled the plate towards him and began to cut a slice. Half-way through the knife stuck.

'Hallo,' said Uncle Ned. 'What's this?' He poked in the cake with the point of the knife and something tinkled down on to the plate.

It was Mummy's silver thimble!

'Well,' said Uncle Ned, eating up all the crumbs he had made, 'I've had cherry cake and coffee cake and seed cake, but this is the first time I've ever had Thimble Cake! Jolly good it is, too!'

BOOTS

It was the night before Christmas Eve, and Mary Kate and Mummy and Daddy were going to stay with Mary Kate's other Granny and Grandad, who lived a long way away. It had been snowing for two days and two nights and while they were having breakfast Daddy said, 'I think the roads are too bad for us to go by car. We shall have to go by train. We can't get to London in time for the morning train, so we shall have to travel tonight.'

Mary Kate was very excited. She had never been in a train at night before.

In the afternoon they went to London and had tea with Auntie Dot and Uncle Ned. After tea Mummy undressed Mary Kate and took her upstairs. She put her in Auntie Dot's big bed with Teddy and a hot-water bottle in a red woolly jacket.

Mary Kate curled herself up small and tried hard to go to sleep but everything was so strange and different from her own little room at home that she just couldn't.

There was a lamp in the street outside and it shone through a gap in the curtains. Every time a car went by a long broom of light swept across the ceiling and showed Mary Kate all the interesting things in Auntie Dot's room ... the china cats on the mantelpiece, the gilt frame on the mirror, the bottles and jars on the dressing-table and the picture of Uncle Ned on the chest of drawers.

At last Mummy came upstairs and took Mary Kate down to the kitchen. She had a drink of warm milk and three biscuits. Then Mummy dressed her in her coat and hat over her pyjamas and wrapped her in a big coloured blanket.

Auntie Dot carried her to the street door. It was quite dark and the stars were out and there were lights in the houses across the road. In some of the windows there were Christmas trees, gay and sparkling bright.

Uncle drove up in his little green car to take them to the station. Daddy took Mary Kate on his knee in the front, Mummy climbed into the back seat with the two bags and the suitcase. They waved 'Good-bye' to Auntie Dot and off they went.

The train was already at the platform when they arrived at the station, huffing and puffing and eager to be off. Mary Kate was very surprised when Daddy carried her into their compartment. It wasn't at all like the ones she was used to. It had four beds in it – bunks, Daddy called them. There were two down low and two up high. Daddy put Mary Kate on one of the bottom bunks and Uncle Ned put the case on one of the top ones.

'I'll sleep in the other top bunk,' said Daddy, 'and Mummy can sleep on the other bottom one.'

'Are we going to bed, then?' asked Mary Kate. 'I thought we were going to travel all night.'

'So we are,' said Mummy, 'but we're going to bed, just the same. You're already undressed, so as soon as I've made up your bunk, in you go!'

'I'll *never* be able to sleep,' sighed Mary Kate. 'I thought I could sit and look out of the window and see the night going by.'

Daddy laughed. 'You wouldn't be able to see much,' he said. 'It's too dark.'

'Never mind,' said Uncle Ned, pulling something from under his coat. 'I've been to get something to keep you cosy,' and he gave her Auntie Dot's hot-water bottle, which a kind lady on the station had filled for him.

Mary Kate snuggled down in the bunk with the hot-water bottle and Teddy. 'Good night, Uncle Ned,' she said. 'I'll just have a little nap till the train starts,' and she closed her eyes.

Soon there was a great deal of puffing and chuffing, the guard blew his whistle and the train began to move slowly out of the station. Faster and faster it went through the snowy night towards the faraway place where Granny and Grandad lived – but Mary Kate didn't know anything about it. She was fast asleep.

When she woke up it was morning and the train was pulling into a big station. Mummy and Daddy were already dressed and drinking tea out of their flasks. Daddy gave Mary Kate some of his tea because his had sugar in it and Mummy gave her two biscuits. Then she scrambled out of the bunk and Mummy dressed her. While Daddy folded up the blankets Mummy repacked her overnight bag and then they were ready to go.

Mummy took Mary Kate across the platform to the cloakroom. 'You can have a proper wash when we get to Granny's,' she said as she wiped

Mary Kate's face and hands with a damp sponge.

Grandad arrived on the platform as they came out of the cloakroom. 'Come along, come along,' he said briskly. 'I've got the car outside. It's snowing hard and we don't want to stand about in the cold, do we?'

Mary Kate sat in the back of the big car with Mummy and Teddy and she was so excited she could hardly speak.

As they drove out of the station yard a black cat ran across the road in front of them. Grandad slowed down and put his head out of the window to look at it.

'I thought for a minute that was our old Boots,' he said, 'but it isn't. Boots has got four white feet. That cat's only got three.'

'Boots wouldn't be all the way up here, surely?' said Daddy, in surprise.

'We don't know *where* he is,' said Grandad sadly. 'He disappeared four days ago.'

'Oh, dear,' said Mummy. 'I *am* sorry. I do hope he'll come back soon.'

Mary Kate hoped so too. She very much wanted to see Granny's black cat with the four white feet.

They drove through the snowy countryside for a

long, long way and Mary Kate began to feel rather empty inside. At last, half-way up a steep hill, the car turned aside into a drive, and there was Granny's house and there was Granny at the front door to welcome them.

She hugged Mary Kate and took her into the house. There was a lovely smell of bacon and eggs and coffee. 'Breakfast straight away,' said Granny, unfastening Mary Kate's coat.

'Mmm,' thought Mary Kate, smelling the breakfast smell. 'I'm going to like staying with this Granny.'

By tea-time she felt as though she had always lived in Granny's house, though she didn't really remember the last time she had been there because she had been so small. She trotted about the big kitchen helping Granny to set the table. The curtains were drawn, the lamps were lit and the kettle was singing softly on the stove. Granny brought in a crusty loaf and cut it up. She put the slices into a little basket for Mary Kate to take into the sitting-room, where Mummy and Daddy and Grandad were dozing by the fire.

'Granny says will you make some toast, please,' said Mary Kate, holding out the basket.

Daddy took the two long, shiny brass toasting forks down from their hooks at the side of the fireplace and he and Mummy knelt on the rug in front of the fire to make the toast.

Mary Kate went back to the kitchen to finish setting the table. Granny was just counting out the spoonfuls of tea into the big brown teapot when there came a scratching noise at the window.

'It's Boots!' cried Granny. 'I'm sure it's Boots! He always scratches on the window when he wants to come in!'

She ran quickly to the outside door and opened it. The wind blew in a flurry of snowflakes and sent the door-curtain billowing into the room. 'Boots! Boots! Boots!' cried Granny into the darkness, but Boots didn't come. At last Granny closed the door and came sadly back to the kitchen.

'Never mind, Granny,' said Mary Kate. 'I'm sure Boots will come back in time for Christmas.'

'He'll have to hurry up, then,' said Granny. 'It's Christmas Day tomorrow. Now, if your mother and father have finished making that toast we'll have our tea.'

Soon after tea Mummy put Mary Kate to bed in Granny's little blue bedroom. 'This is where your

Daddy used to sleep,' said Mummy. 'There's a balcony outside the window and an apple tree that he used to climb when he was a boy.'

Mary Kate hung up her stocking at the foot of the bed and Mummy tucked her in and kissed her 'Good night'. Then she opened the window a little bit, drew back the curtains and went downstairs.

Mary Kate soon went to sleep, but it wasn't long before she woke up again. Something was moving about at the bottom of the bed.

'It's Father Christmas!' thought Mary Kate. 'I wonder if he'll put the light on? It's so dark I can't see him.'

She lay quite still and listened. There wasn't a sound. Through the window she could see the low winter stars, very big and bright.

Suddenly, from the bottom of the bed came a rumbly noise.

Mary Kate sat up. 'I know what that noise is,' she said to herself. She moved her feet very gently. The noise stopped. Then something sat on her legs. Mary Kate laughed and put out her hand and touched it.

'I know who *you* are,' she said and called out loudly, 'Granny! Granny! Grannee-ee-ee!'

Up the stairs came Granny and opened the bedroom door. The light from the hanging lamp on the landing shone across the bedroom and there, in the middle of Mary Kate's bed, was Boots!

'Good gracious me,' cried Granny. 'He must have come up the apple tree, on to the balcony and in through the window!'

'Just as I used to,' said Daddy, coming in to see what all the noise was about.

Granny lifted Boots off the bed. 'I hope he didn't frighten you, Mary Kate.'

'Oh, no,' said Mary Kate. 'I thought he was Father Christmas!'

Daddy laughed. 'Perhaps he is,' he said. 'After all, you never can tell with cats, can you – especially black ones.' He tucked Mary Kate in snug and warm. 'Sleep now, poppet,' he said. 'Stockings don't get filled while children are awake, whether they're filled by Santa Claus or Pussycat Claws. Good night now.' And he closed the door and went downstairs.

The author

Helen Morgan was born in 1921, and became a book-worm as soon as she learned to read. When she was twelve she lost her sight, but it partially returned a year later. As her parents had forbidden reading, she had to read secretly by lamplight or candlelight. She made up stories and wrote poetry, and before she was fifteen she had written two novels, which her father burnt because she was so bad at all her school subjects except English and cooking.

Her father died when she was seventeen, and she was trained as a shorthand typist at a school for the blind, though she could never read Braille fast enough to enjoy it. She went on writing stories, but did not have any encouragement until she married in 1954, when her husband bought her a typewriter. She now has three daughters, and her husband helps her with the house as much as possible to give her time to write. She dislikes housework, noise, and knitting, and enjoys listening to music and radio and television plays.

Helen Morgan has also written *The Little Old Lady* and *Tales of Tigg's Farm*.

Also in Young Puffins are *Mary Kate and the School Bus* and *Mrs Pinny and the Blowing Day*.

Also by Helen Morgan

MARY KATE AND THE SCHOOL BUS

Mary Kate is five now, and more than ready for school with all its grown-up new interests.

MRS PINNY AND THE BLOWING DAY

Washday – and a windy magic blows over Mrs Pinny, her washing, and even the local train service.

Some other Young Puffins

THE DOLLS' HOUSE
Rumer Godden

Mr and Mrs Plantaganet and their family were very happy in their antique dolls' house, until Marchpane the elegant, selfish china doll moved in with them and acted as if she owned the place.

A GIFT FROM WINKLESEA
Helen Cresswell

Dan and Mary buy a beautiful stone like an egg as a present for their mother – and then it hatches out, into the oddest animal they ever saw.

THE STORY OF HOLLY AND IVY
Rumer Godden

A magical Christmas story about three special wishes made by a lonely little orphan girl, a doll without an owner, and a policeman's wife with no child to share her Christmas tree.

THE YOUNG PUFFIN BOOK OF VERSE
Barbara Ireson

A deluge of poems about such fascinating subjects as birds and balloons, mice and moonshine, farmers and frogs, pigeons and pirates, especially chosen to please young people of four to eight. (*Original*)

UMBRELLA THURSDAY and A HELPING HAND
Janet McNeill

Good deeds sometimes have funny results, as the two little girls in these stories discover.

MILLY-MOLLY-MANDY STORIES
FURTHER DOINGS OF MILLY-MOLLY-MANDY
MILLY-MOLLY-MANDY AGAIN
MORE OF MILLY-MOLLY-MANDY

Joyce Lankester Brisley

Well-known and well-loved stories of a little girl growing up in a country village, at the heart of a busy, happy family.

THE TALES OF OLGA DA POLGA

Michael Bond

Michael Bond's latest heroine is an enchantingly independent guinea-pig with a zest for adventure. (*Original*)

DEAR TEDDY ROBINSON
ABOUT TEDDY ROBINSON
TEDDY ROBINSON HIMSELF
KEEPING UP WITH TEDDY ROBINSON

Joan G. Robinson

Teddy Robinson was Deborah's teddy bear and such a very nice, friendly cuddly bear that he went everywhere with her and had even more adventures than she did. Perfect bedtime reading for four-year-olds.

LITTLE OLD MRS PEPPERPOT
MRS PEPPERPOT TO THE RESCUE

Alf Prøysen

Gay little stories about an old woman who suddenly shrinks to the size of a pepperpot.